this Book
belongs to:
_____

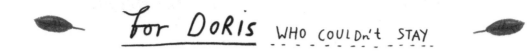

_For Doris_ WHO couLDn't STAY

I STILL see YOUR green EYES in all THE leaves.

'Deeper meaning resides in the fairy tales told to me
in my childhood than in the truth that is taught in life.'
— Friedrich Schiller

_Leaf_ is © Flying Eye Books 2017.

This is a first edition published in 2017 by Flying Eye Books,
an imprint of Nobrow Ltd. 27 Westgate Street, London E8 3RL.

Text and illustrations © Sandra Dieckmann 2017.
Sandra Dieckmann has asserted her right under the Copyright, Designs and
Patents Act, 1988, to be identified as the Author and Illustrator of this Work.

Published in the US by Nobrow (US) Inc.
Printed in Latvia on FSC® certified paper.
ISBN: 978-1-911171-31-7

Order from www.flyingeyebooks.com

# Leaf

BY SANDRA DIECKMANN

Flying Eye Books

London | New York

Crow saw it first. The strange white creature,
carried upon the dark waves towards the shore.

It was unlike anything the animals of
the wild wood had seen before. It made its
home in the old, overgrown cave on the hill.

No one had lived there for as long as they could
remember, and no one dared approach now.

Stomping around the forest, the creature collected leaves every day.
Big leaves and small leaves, round leaves and colourful ones.

As he looked around the forest with
a searching eye, the animals would flee in fear.

RUN!

They named him LEAF, not only after the creature's
odd habit, but because they wanted him to leave.
No one, they thought, should have to live in fear.

Every day they discussed the stranger,
but no one was brave enough to talk to him.

One day, fox called out to the other
animals as Leaf burst through the forest.
He ran very fast and was covered
in hundreds of beautiful leaves.
They had NEVER seen anything like it!

Look!

With a giant... ROOOAR!

...Leaf leaped off the edge of the hill and flew...

...for a moment at least, before tumbling down into the lake.

Soaking wet, the beast stomped back to hide once again in the dark cave.

A meeting was called to decide what to do about this strange situation. The crows suggested talking to him,

but everyone looked to the ground and shook their heads.
So they decided nothing – only that they didn't agree!

A few days passed, and Leaf burst out of the cave again. This time he didn't stop running at the hill, but ran all the way through the wild wood to the edge of the great cliff. He jumped off and flew...

The sea spat him out just like the day he arrived.
Only now the clever crows decided it was
time to talk to the very sad and lonely Leaf.
They let him speak and at last they all listened.

Leaf told them how he had drifted over from far across
the sea, where the ice was melting. After all, he was only
a polar bear wanting to go back to his family.

Just someone who wished he could fly back home.
How silly they had all been for not talking to him sooner!

And so it was decided. The crows would help Leaf and fly him home...

...and the animals promised to tell Leaf's story to everyone who would listen, so that no polar bear would ever get lost again.